— K.P. KULSKI —

HOUSE OF PUNGSU

ISBN: 978-1-68510-061-2 (sc)
ISBN: 978-1-68510-062-9 (ebook)

First printing edition: September 30, 2022
Printed by Bizarro Pulp Press in the United States of America.
Cover Design and Layout: Don Noble
Edited by Erin Al-Mehairi
Proofreading and Interior Layout by Scarlett R. Algee

Bizarro Pulp Press, an imprint of JournalStone Publishing
3205 Sassafras Trail
Carbondale, Illinois 62901

Bizarro Pulp Press books may be ordered through booksellers or by contacting:

JournalStone | www.journalstone.com

For Omma,
who taught me
the true meaning
of the Tiger

HOUSE OF PUNGSU

My soul is wind and water and the tiger has taught me to run—away from the stillness and expectations.

With instinctual greed I grip this freedom. For too long, womanhood has been the carving of the woman—prime slices for the feast of others. I am so tired of dwindling. I am so furious at the self-sacrifice. I am tired of regret.

"Breathe fire," she tells me.

"How?" I ask, considering the possibilities in desperate glee.

She smiles. "First step," her hand ushers me forward and she lowers her voice. "The first step is the dying." Before I am aware of anything, she shoves me hard—

and I fall, like a star cast out of a false heaven. I watch the shadow of leaves formed by the setting sun poking through the trees.

I think of walls.

I think about being contained.

Then I reject it all.

Before the end, there must be a journey.

And this story—is *my* journey.

DAUGHTER

It is a palace in the style of the Korean Joseon kings; a great walled collection of elaborate halls and pavilions, cobbled courtyards, and man-made reflecting pools. A stronghold of decisions, regal processions, important officials—except it has none of these things. Only the structures, walls, and three people in total who dwell within.

Daughter, Mother, Grandmother.

It is here that I learned who I am. What I want. To reject old values. Some might say it was too late to learn, but really, it was the perfect time and place for such lessons.

It begins with menstruation; the blood seeps from the wound of womanhood and I can't remember a time this has happened—to menstruate, to be in a state of change. Not here. Things here don't change.

A world of immutability, so still that the lake's waters seem frozen into an eternal mirror. A liquid alternate-reality where the streaks of orange and yellow from the setting sun contrast with the clouded blue mountains. They seem bigger in the lake's vision, as if the heavens push down instead of soaring. A heavy fall that crashes upon the rooftop of Imjin Pavilion.

Or perhaps, I am seeing it all wrong. Perhaps instead, the crimson-painted pillars of the ambulatory hold up not only the roof, but the heavens as well. In my red hanbok I could be an odd addition to the pillars, another forever silent thing carved from wood, whose only purpose is to be part of the Pavilion, and by extension, the palace.

I have been and will be sixteen forever. I cannot remember a time I've been anything else, or that grandmother and mother had been any other age. I'm well-read enough to know this is strange. There are stories filled with infants and children, of marriages. I understand these things like snapshots of someone's else's life glimpsed through a window. From these stories I gain sustenance, a stream of knowledge and the fantastic.

Funny how the walls are never present in the lake's reflection, how the tops of them always fall below the lake's reflective eye. The lake suggests we pretend that only what it can see be reality, but if that was true, how would anything within the buildings be real? Are our thoughts and hopes real? These questions are maddening, so I rip a fluffy peony head and let the shower of white petals fall upon the liquid surface. Let the lake get a close look at the harshness of existence, let it smell the perfume and taste its beauty, and then, let it be touched with its brutal end.

I can look with my own eyes and see the wall, how thick it sprouts from the dusty ground, towering whitewashed stone. It pretends not to trap us in, looking endless as it runs the length of the large grounds. But I know it turns, runs, and then turns again and again, in sharp angles, jutting and trapping us within. Animals within a gilded cage. A cage that hints there may be something more outside. Mountains in the distance and trees swaying in breezes beyond the wall. An excellent artist must have painted them, because they seem genuine. Just enough embellishment to make the viewer imagine the cool touch of mists upon its tops but never feel them for herself.

And shouldn't I be satisfied existing here? I can almost hear the jailers in my mind. *Look what we have given you. The finest things by the finest creators. Protected, secured, so that we can drain you of all your spirited existence.*

I step under the shadow of the pavilion. The first floor opens to the air, the creamy jade ceiling supported by a forest of columns. In the center of the open space looms a large ornate chair, raised on a dais. A painted screen behind it depicts a view of mountaintops, the same mountains beyond the wall, illuminated by the sun and moon coexisting on opposite edges. Many times, I have wished to climb those steps and sit in the chair—imagined myself on it. But I always stop, chiding myself.

"That is a seat for great men. Not a seat for you."

Why shouldn't it be for me? Even as I reach with my girl-heart for great things, I have learned to slap my own wrist, to stop the dream.

"Wishing for something that cannot be is a waste of time and energy." That is what mother tells me. "It only leads to disappointment."

There lives an animal within me that growls when I hear this, a wild thing that wants to bite its tether, yet I do nothing to free it. Instead, I stand very still, say little, and wait for the fury to subside. But now, I am bleeding as a girl should when coming of age. A womb that has grown to fertility, but I can't help worrying that I have stifled the animal for too long, and that somehow, I managed to kill it and this blood...it is the bleeding of the wildness within me, being squeezed out of my spirit. I am being hollowed out.

***

Within the pavilion, I follow the edges of the lower level, but no matter where I stand the lake can still spot me, morphing my stature into a blurred crimson thing, making it hard to see where I end and where the pavilion begins.

I climb the red staircase to the upper level, hugging my most recent find from the King's extensive library, an entire structure dedicated to the collection and housing of texts from around the world. Like most things here on the palace grounds, the building endures as a mystery. Each visit I find the books shifted and sometimes a new treasure, like this one, added. I don't wonder too much about how this happens anymore, only celebrate that it happens at all. Without the books, I would lose my mind and the last frontier of my freedom, within the realm of stories and knowledge.

As I hoped, the great heavy door to grandmother's quarters has been unbarred for the day and my heart grows happy, looking forward to the time I get to spend with the old woman. I step within, away from the prying eyes of the lake.

Grandmother's room feels less like a room, more like a forest, lush and vibrant. Potted plants envelop every surface, floor to tables. When I come to visit, the plants have moved to new positions, like watchmen coming and going from duty. Tall and leafy saplings, short and frilly ferns, all tendrils of green reaching from all possible directions like chlorophyll penitents hoping to touch my hem. I can scarcely figure the full breadth and width of the space. A brittle woman bound to her bed surrounded by innumerable greenery. She is all sticks, my grandmother, the angles of her face as sharp as her eyes, watching from her forest.

"Wonderful," she says, "you've arrived."

A smile curves my lips, reaching my heart. "I have, and I see you've stayed."

We both laugh, I with my hand covering my mouth, a habit I've been taught because a lady doesn't expose the pink insides of her mouth. I suspect it's really meant to hide my joy, an offensive thing for a girl to maintain. Good training for marriage, mother would say.

"For now, granddaughter, but only because I choose to stay." Her eyes light with a mischievous twinkle, making me slow for a moment and wonder if it was said in jest or seriousness.

"Are you ready for a story today?" she asks.

"Yes, are you?" I say. This is what we do, trade tales, her from memory, and I from the books I find in the library.

"Oh yes," she nods and pats the dark wood floor, where I always sit. One of the few spots unoccupied by growing things.

As I settle beside her, she grabs my hand, knobby joints push into my palm as she squeezes in affection. "Good, good. We are both storytellers, then, in a world of listeners."

I cock my head, considering her words and how odd they sound. No larger world exists for us. We only know the myriad of structures of the palace grounds, walled and cut off from whatever exists out there. I lick my lips, and almost speak these thoughts out loud, but at the last moment I say instead, "We are listeners too."

"Of course, one cannot be a storyteller without having been a listener first." She winks at me. "Now first tell me, how is granddaughter today? Has she found a way to escape the palace yet?"

Are my thoughts so obvious? The leaves of a nearby plant wave up and down ever so slightly, as if laughing at my confusion. I open my mouth to rebuke it, then close it again. Grandmother waits patiently with a grin. She knows me too well. "Have you?" I ask finally and somewhat cautiously, afraid of mother overhearing.

She laughs loud at this, amusement pulled from deep within the withered cave her chest. "You are too clever, too clever. Remember this; if there is a way in, there is a way out."

"What do you mean?" I push but the light in her dims, just a little.

Her lips purse before she brightens again, and she pats my hand.

"I've begun the women's bleed," I say abruptly.

She looks at me with confusion, and then, a quiet nod. "Now that is an odd thing."

"Is it bad? It seems that here in the palace...it shouldn't happen."

"I don't know," she admits. "But what if it is something good? What if there is a reason we cannot grasp yet? Change in the house of no change." Her eyes glitter upon me, thoughtful.

Shifting my weight, I am not so sure. Perhaps it means nothing at all. A quiet passes between us, both keeping internal counsels. The ferns and leaves nearby rustle with the caress of a soft breeze. Breezes in a room with no wind.

Grandmother breaks the silence first. "I have a story that I think you should hear. Are you ready?"

Pushing myself out of reverie, I smile. "Of course, grandmother. I am ready."

***

In the ancient times of Korea, there was a modest woman who lived in a village. One day her husband was called to war. It was his duty to accept the king's call, and so the husband packed up his things and answered the summons. For years he was gone. But his good wife waited for him, longing each day for his return. After a long time, she saw on the mountain path, a worn and tired man walking toward her home. In joy, she recognized her husband and received him happily.

The war was over, but the man she married had changed. He no longer smiled. His lips held in a perpetual angry slash, like a crack that opened only to drink soju at all hours of the day. His once youthful face had turned sallow, but the worst was what changed on the inside and what he did with that change. He was cruel and filled with fury that vomited upon her with torrential abuse.

The wife cowered in the corners of their small home, never knowing when the next blow from his fists would come. This is how she came to fear him. Yet, beneath it all, the woman could sense a great wound, a sadness her husband did not discuss. After many months of unhappiness, the woman went to see a wise man in the village for help. She no longer knew how she could live with the darkness that consumed her husband.

On her journey to the wise man's house, she wept, all the while afraid that someone would hear her, but the tears needed to come forth, demanded to be acknowledged. She stopped to sit on a large boulder, and as she rested, her tears fell like morning dew upon the dusty soil. Only grandfather mountain saw her tears and rumbled gently in sympathy.

Soon, the wife reached the wise man's straw-thatched house. A surge of hope grew in her chest at the sight of the house. Surely, the wise man would help her.

***

Grandmother stops and smiles; most of her teeth are missing, but a beautiful thing to see just the same. "Now what do you think about that?" she asks, tilting her chin to her chest.

I want to think of something clever, but this beginning irritates me; it seems obvious what the woman should do. But anyone who's heard folktales knows that the characters don't always act logically, as if they are bound by invisible threads of the story itself, rules that we accept but don't understand. Rules that ring hollow when challenged.

"It seems she should talk to her husband and ask him what is wrong," I say with a shrug. It seems simple enough. Why wouldn't the woman do that? Perhaps the man was ashamed, and she sensed it? But why would she put his pride over her own safety? I shake my head. So much in these stories could be solved by some perspective change. Or breaking the rules of the story. Perhaps the wife should become a woman with a name instead of an association. An identity that belongs to her and her alone.

Grandmother nods as if she hears my thoughts. Her eyes study me, sharply absorbing every pull of my facial muscles. We sit for a moment in silence, her eyes looking into mine. Sometimes I hope she will tell me what she sees—what part of me is important, worth cultivating.

Grandmother seems to come to some sort of a decision. She squeezes my hand once. "Well then, I will tell you more next time. Since I have given you a story, it is time for you to give me one."

"Unfair," I say and pretend to protest, trying to tease her mood to something lighter, "only part of a story in trade for a whole one?"

A chuckle wheezes from her lips and she presses herself back into the pillows. She looks tired suddenly. "I am old and eccentric, now read the story for me."

I pretend to sigh, but I'm just searching her face for clues of what she's thinking. As usual, her wrinkles are maps of her experiences, but not her thoughts.

She watches my hands as I page through, playing with the bits of ribbon that mark our favorites. "What shall I read today, then?" I ask, and wonder if she'll go for a pretty tale, the versions that end in neat packages.

"The one with the little girl in red, lost in the woods," she says.

"She wasn't lost, she was on her way to her grandmother's house," I say. For some reason I feel defensive of Little Red.

Grandmother waves a hand at me. "Just read, lost granddaughter in red."

I rock with a satisfied huff and nod, letting my amusement show. She usually loves the bloody ones best, and this one is no different. Stepsisters slicing their feet so that they could shape their bodies into the mold of glass set out for them and old women eaten up by wolves; every time these stories end, grandmother laughs, a throaty gusto of joy. I can't figure what amuses her so much about these tales. To me, they are horrifying, but her laughter is infectious, and I usually end laughing too. Deep amusement over the sorrows of these characters locked in their story cycle of forever.

Will Little Red be forever traveling to her grandmother's house? Forever staring at the horror of the wolf?

***

Before the darkness has a chance to emerge, I light candles in each room, working from the bottom floor and moving up the stairway, into the upper level where the shadows feel longest. The burning of so many little flames emanates a soft heat of its own. The pavilion was not constructed for daily living, but to house flexible spaces for official functions, changing to fit any need. An echo of memory lives here, and as I pass, things shift within as if restless. Sliding rice paper doors, light in their grooves, wood caressing wood as they glide and stop. Corridors transform into banquet and receiving rooms. Only three rooms do not change like this. Grandmother and mother's rooms on the upper level, and mine, a room just off the kitchen on the lower level. Perhaps this explains why we reside here in this pavilion. There are others on the grounds, all with the same shifting walls, beautiful works of art in constant rearrangement. But Imjin Pavilion belongs to us. Besides, I've been warned to never enter any other buildings except for the library. Pavilions and halls that remain closed to me. To keep me from finding...what exactly? From the discovery of rice paper walls and mahogany beams?

Mother meets me in the hallway as I emerge on the upper floor, her eyes dark pools, black hair filaments of shadow. She moves to the door of grandmother's room. There she secures the great heavy door, pulling at latches and bolts, five in total and a heavy wood bar. This ritual happens every day at sunset and I've long since stopped asking questions. She glances down at me, the fading sun golden on her proud features. "Go, daughter," she says, "the day is ending." On cue, the sun falls below the hall window and I dutifully do as I'm told.

As I leave, I hear a compliment of locks also sliding on the opposite side of the door, a seemingly impossible thing because grandmother has been bedridden for as long as I can remember. I've heard the locks many times before, but it sets my mind alight with intense curiosity, a desire to see the other side before the shadows take hold and I shove it down. Then I think I hear a bird call within, but all falls quiet, leaving me listening only to the settling wood. Grandmother's door is the only interior one fashioned of heavy wood and hinged, except, of course, the entry door that leads out of the pavilion. This door, like the palace gates, is made to keep people from entering. Or perhaps, to keep people within. I am not sure the true purpose of either, because I cannot leave the palace grounds any more than grandmother can leave her room at night.

***

There's another girl who walks through a fairy tale life. Not the clean stories, but the dark ones, the ones where women bleed to fit into containers. In my dreams, I am one of those women, but I don't want to be one of those women. Rules that hold me in and hold me back. Rumors of dangers just beyond my awareness. The knowledge that there are things that move in the darkness, but I cannot know their intent, cannot ascertain their desires.

I exist just beyond the haze of smoke; the tinkling of ornaments in my hair obscures my words. This time I am seated on the dais I covet; a screen divides the room between me and officials. They are important. I am important too. Hushed voices murmur, the sounds of a thousand whispers drilling into my mind like worms.

"She must," one official intones to another. The room echoes with his words, moving like a sseunami, growing more powerful with each wave.

"She can't," the other replies, his tall black yangban hat bowing with his words. The sseunami gains momentum, strength, and I feel as if it drains out of my body as it passes through me.

"I can," I shout, morphing into a shriek, a desperate assertion. They don't seem to hear. The man beside me claps a hand on my arm. I know he should protect me, but I also know stories warn us how those who should protect are all too often the ones who cause the most grievous wounds. My arm burns in response, and I look down as rusted iron envelopes the flesh of his hand, each finger a blade piercing my softness, biting, and drawing wells of deep red-black blood. "I gave you worth," he says. I cannot see his face. But it no longer matters, because suddenly, the screen between us and the yangban erupts into flame.

***

When I wake, she is suspended over me again, a woman I cannot recognize. She stares with what's left of her eyes. Watching me in dumbfounded pain, face blistered and charred by fire. Her fine hanbok forms stiff adhesions to her battered body. Where the fire hasn't touched her flesh are purple bruises and welts, lacerations that weep pus. She opens her mouth and opens her legs and out rushes blood, so much dark blood. It rains over me in hot splatters. I taste copper and bitterness.

I taste the earth.

MOTHER

Daughter is young. I watch her and see only innocence and persimmon-sticky hands. Lips that want for treats and avoid the bitter things. She's lost and I worry she will fade away into smoke and I will forget that she even existed at all.

Funny how we build our own hells, the prisons we erect from grooves of our passing to and fro, until the road no longer exists, but only a hall framed with impossible walls.

We build these things because we love.

Love leads to worry and how we shape our worlds trying to prevent pain, suffering...death. Love leads to duty, stability. Even the hope of love does these things.

I smooth my hair into a low, tight bun and let my hands fall. The lake stares with my eyes, large and full of a collection of hurts.

This palace hides secrets. I hide secrets.

***

The morning air falls cool across my skin and the accursed lake gapes at the rising sun with a single wide eye, pulling in the brightness and turning itself in a dazzling jewel. As I do most mornings, I rise and leave the pavilion for the greater palace grounds. Wood is piled along the north wall, so I head there, kicking up white-gray gravel and dust. The eaves of the other pavilions are a riot of deep color, reds and golds, azure blues that are so intense that they seem supernatural. The tips of the tiled roofs lift at the corners, as if smiling in greeting. Just beyond, a large pavilion looms, its roof coming to a point as if readying itself to spear the sun. White figures adorn the top, but I can never see exactly what they are. I am drawn to the stone steps and the white doors, but I force myself to pass. To block out the memories. Yet sometimes, I think the memories possess me, take control of my body.

The wall rises before me, and how I hate it. To think there may be a world just beyond its stones. I lean into its shadow, pressing my ear and cheek to the chill of the stone. A great dead thing, a carcass of petrified death of long-ago creatures and ancient oceans, all made hard and devoid of identity.

Would they sing if they still knew themselves? Primordial creatures of Earth's first beatings of life. Bacteria long buried along with the bones of the mammoths. All their little pieces compressed or fired into something so devoid of warmth. They all had stories to tell.

With a sigh, I pull away to work on gathering wood. Piling as many as I can handle onto the leather carrying harness, I strap the collection to my back, leaning forward so that I am not bent backwards like a willow. I've fallen backwards before and been quite humbled, learning the perspective of a beetle stuck on its back, wrangling in desperation to regain its feet. The wall seems unimpressed, and I scoff internally.

For so long I have been buried here, static, locked into place. Once there had been hope and the possibility of the future. These things carved away with small, precise cuts. All that has been, all that I could have been, will turn to stone just like the ones embedded into the wall.

There was a man who used to live in the palace. A man who held the keys to it all, who wouldn't let me forget. Once he made me open each door; how heavy those keys felt in my hand. How small I felt holding them. Clicks of locks released are echoes of a warning, the first sign of danger. I did not know yet, but he was sure to show me, to make me see the things within.

The pain still stains my soul, the images burn, and I sometimes I can see their faces. How quickly I threw that door shut, locking it with such commitment I believed it would never be opened again. He had me do this a hundred times, until every key had been used and every hall or pavilion had been looked into with my own eyes.

I know the contents of this place. I will never forget what lurks just beyond. With all that I was, I swore to myself I would keep the doors sealed.

"Uncomfortable truths make for uncomfortable hiding places," he had told me. Then he kissed me, lonely long kisses, and put a child in my womb that will never be born.

Now I am the bearer of the keys, the guardian of the secrets I never want to remember. Yet somehow, for the first time in memory, a key goes missing. The heavy metal of it has abandoned me.

No longer is there room for daydreams or romantic thoughts.

I walk the palace in the night with my lantern, locking the doors, checking them over and over until I can think of nothing else but the slide of bolts in their sockets and the jangle of keys against my heart.

If only I can find it again.

If only I can forget.

Something has changed. I can feel a charge in the air. The coming of something I cannot name.

***

"What if one day, you must guard this place?" I tell my daughter as I slice garlic. Let her think the tears in my eyes are from the pungent fumes of my work. Not from regret and worry and hopelessness.

Perplexed, she gawks at me, a fish sucking at air. "Where will you be?"

"You can't expect me to always be here." I stop slicing and study her. Trying to see how my words fall upon her heart and mind. I can see her think about this, as it has never occurred to her that I would cease to exist. She needs to be tougher, stronger, in order to live this kind of existence. Chama, I want to say to her. *Endure.*

"What about grandmother? Won't she be gone too then?"

"Perhaps," I say, trying to curve my lips kindly, but the bitterness has sapped my ability. I probably look worse for trying. But it still hurts to be so easily cast aside, to be taken for granted. It's been too long since anyone has seen me and not the hands that keep order. I will never close the gap between us like that, but a part of me knows I never will be able to. I can't take care of both her and grandmother, while being a friend. I can only mother, the perpetual labor of responsibility and sacrifice. The work of this place must still happen even if it makes daughter hate me. Yet somehow, I must remember the joy too, but so often the feeling escapes me.

"How?" Her brows furrow, wrinkling her forehead.

"You must be strong," I say, and regret the words the moment they leave my mouth. I once had hope and ideas that things could be different, at least for me.

I try to drop my brows, relax my worry. Perhaps things *will* be different for her. She bleeds as if she lives normally. *Normal.* The word sours in my imagination and I scowl. She probably thinks the expression is for her, so I try to even out my features quickly before she takes note.

"I don't understand," she almost whispers, as if she's afraid to tell me. Afraid of the meaning. I cannot comfort her because I will not lie to her. All I can do is tell her things bit by bit, the right amount to grab and digest. I want to tell her I love her. The words get caught inside of a trap in my throat, a cage that makes me feel like I will drown in my hopes for her. How do I ask her to break free of this place, all the while preparing her for the likeliness that she will be trapped here forever, just as I am?

I put down a bowl filled with hot food; it says all the things I can't. *I love you. I care. I want you to be free.* But those words are silent promises. The ones I can vocalize are filled with action, purpose. "You don't need to understand. Now eat. You'll need your strength."

DAUGHTER

The wildness within me bites and writhes, turning my insides into a mass of aches, rolling forward in dull pain ebbing away and returning. I shift uncomfortably, the wad of rags stuffed into my undergarments continually soaking up the blood that falls from me, a mudslide in too much rain. Mother should know, I should tell her. She will be afraid. Perhaps not without merit, who knows what it portends? A rite of passage, a new phase of what exactly? For us here in the pavilion, it may mean nothing, or it may mean everything.

Mother enters and I look up; her eyes are pools of worry, hard with the exertion of sleepless nights. I turn away wordlessly, tending to the kitchen hearth, fanning the flames so that the vent behind it will pull the heat under the floorboards and warm the pavilion. It doesn't really need much; the palace exists in an eternal spring. There are times I wonder why we bother with heat at all. Or even food and drink. What if we were to stop these things, would we wither or stay the same?

"When did it start?" Mother says, and I can feel her watching me.

"The bleed?" I know what she's asking, but I'm trying to understand why the edge of her voice tinges with...surprise? Alarm? I can't be sure. Of course, she would know. She knows all that happens on the palace grounds.

"Yes, that."

For the briefest of moments, the flames of the dream return as I watch the hearth lick up, dancing in my vision. I hesitate, willing the kitchen to return to focus, and straighten my back. "I don't know, a day, perhaps two ago."

Hands disappear into her sleeves as if her fingers clench involuntarily. "This makes no sense."

"Why?" I ask innocently, trying to remember, grasping for clarity, a picture of my childhood. I've always been this age, and at this place. Except, I know somehow that isn't the truth. Before I had grown up, been a child, been places other than here. Then the knowledge flicks away and I cannot see it any longer.

"Makes no sense," she says again, shaking her head this time.

Her hands pop back out of her sleeves and she steps toward me, capturing my gaze with hers. Her eyes are blackness in the shadows, a dark empty space, pupils opened so wide pulling at everything in the hope of filling the hollowness. "Daughter." The word escapes her mouth like a sigh. "Those of us here. We aren't supposed to do anything like others. We don't menstruate. We don't—we can't bleed."

We can't bleed.

The words seep into my mind like cracks through granite. Not just menstruation—I've never seen any of us cut, no red smears from scratches, or even welts from bruised knees. "What do you think it means?" I ask.

"I don't know."

She is beautiful, my mother, even with the shadows that live in her eyes. Not that her beauty has brought her any happiness. She exists as a lark without a song, lovely moth destined to consume nothing but give birth to worry. A statue. A thing that I can only wish would be real, a representation of my hopes, even at times an inspiration. Yet ultimately, nothing about her warms me.

"Yet, I *am* bleeding."

She holds my gaze with her own; her features don't move, as if carved from ivory.

"Have you ever tried to leave?" I ask suddenly, the words slipping out before I could stop them.

A flicker in those eyes, a movement of emotion...despair? "We can't," she says, her voice emotionless, reciting a rule of nature, an unalterable truth. I can't be sure of its wrongness.

A rain begins outside, a whooshing drop of water from the heavens all at once. It clatters on against the courtyard tiles just outside the kitchen door, the sound taking up the space where our conversation had been. Mother looks outside in astonishment. My heart leaps into my chest. Here in the palace, we don't bleed, and it does not rain.

We wander into the courtyard; raindrops fall from the sky in a constant pitter-patter and I hold my hands up to catch. Letting it soak my hair and clothes, and not long after, the rag in my underwear. A tiny, diluted red river trickles from a leg, joining with the liquid cosmos, following small ephemeral streams to the low point of the courtyard, the center, where the Rose of Sharon tree grows. Soon the blood and water are drunk up by the soil; later the tree will drink too.

***

Tonight, the sounds coming from grandmother's room are primal. Low growls and sniffing, scratches on the wood. Shrieks and howls, the scrape of furniture, the beat of rain hitting leaves, and voices.

Then the drums begin. A steady rhythm that takes up residence in my mind, short-circuiting the flow of thoughts until I sleep. Tonight's dreamland is carnage.

There are no screens with men passing judgment. This time, I'm standing on a field with war drums in the distance. I am surrounded by the dead and dying. Some wail, others only gurgle, and the still ones are quickly turning waxy and stiff. They reach for me, begging for reprieve and relief of their pain. I pull back, horrified, unwilling to let their death touch the hem of my chima.

I see the source. She dances in the epicenter of it all, long gray hair swaying as she slays. Men in banded mail, curved swords held aloft, and she kills them all with a flick of her fingers as if her appendages are made of knives instead of flesh. It's grandmother. She laughs as she kills, power coursing through her wrinkled flesh.

When she sees me, she quiets. Then she opens her mouth, and from it a roar comes forth with a boom. But I hear her words in the animal voice. She's asking me a question with a wry smile. I am waking, so I stretch toward her, straining to hear the syllables, make out the variations of sound.

Suddenly, I am pulled through the tunnel to the waking world, but her voice follows me and finally I can hear it in the whoosh of my consciousness, make out the words. "Now what do you think about that?"

***

When I wake, I am alone. There's no burned woman waiting to greet me with her wounds. In her stead is an iron key, left like an offering on my floor.

***

I take five steps toward the throne room and stop in shock. A broken world greets my view. Priceless vases of green porcelain, stamped with the names of expert potters, are no more than shards on the floor. Fine cherry wood tables and cabinets overturned, some splintered. I stare, soundlessly. How could have this occurred mere steps from where I slept?

A creak and a sharp intake of breath tells me mother has arrived. "What happened?" Her voice turns iron but also filled with regret, asking as if I had answers.

I can't speak at first; my tongue thickens in my mouth.

"Do you hear me? What happened here?" Heat enters her voice. I can see the dead at my feet again, grandmother dancing in the center of it all. Destroying.

"I don't know," I manage to stammer.

She stares at the fragments too, and there's something else, a puffiness in her face, faint stains of red. She's been crying, I realize.

"Clean it up," mother says.

And I do.

I sweep the shards, right furniture. The broken porcelain saddens me the most, stamped with the names of potters who've spent their lives in the pursuit of art. Here are only shards left of their labors, bits and pieces. Fragments of a particular favorite, its insides glare white glaze, startling. I study it closely, as if the white were cracked bones, the secret inner workings that once formed the whole. Scratched onto the white are words. I snatch up the fragment and without understanding why, stash it into my pockets.

The air hums with energy as if the palace watches and passes judgment upon me. Why should I not take it? Is there a law? The same unspoken law that doesn't allow us to leave. I am tired of rules that seem to exist only as mechanisms of constraint.

Broken pieces vibrate where they lie, turning hazy, edges less solid. The piece I gathered answers with its own vibration through my pocket. Each fragment slides toward its broken mates, mending themselves. Vase after vase, pieces of furniture—all the broken pieces, splinters and shards disappear into objects of recognition. Beautiful and useful once again, they fly back to the places where they sat. Except one. One vase whose shard remains in my pocket, unable to become whole. Pieced back together, but without the final shard, this one vase remains tragically undone.

I don't return it. Don't choose to give it back. I decide the shard belongs to me, a jagged edge of broken that I keep to myself.

***

Escape. The idea haunts me, hangs in the air, and overlays everything in the palace. Possibility cracks open doorways, glimpses of a light so brilliant I cannot look away. I do the only thing I can think of: I run, pushing myself out of the streets and alleyways of the complex, first through the interior entry gates. The dazzling white paving stones meet me on the other side, cutting through the framed space to the exterior gate like a causeway constructed over a sea of emptiness. I push my legs harder. I am so close. The goal looming before me.

Stumbling, I land on my knees hard and the pain jolts through my body, burning my awareness. But I'm already up again and the exterior gate is so close—the huge red doors that mark the extent of our existence. There must be something on the other side and I must see it. Must escape into it.

White lines of white road, a bridge to possibility. I fall onto the gate door with a thump, gasping for breath, hair tumbling about my face in raven disarray. The key? Shaped metal, this key could have been a sword or a cooking pot. Perhaps an ax claiming dominion over wood. Yet it is none of those things, only a slab of metal with one function, to fit into a lock. Pots and axes, perhaps they lament they are not keys. Or the key laments that it cannot be a sword.

The great heavy doors don't want to yield, but they have no choice. The need to know overwhelms me. I push the key to the deegut-shaped lock. Iron to iron. The stem of the key slides, its teeth biting to the appropriate spaces, and I feel the acceptance of it. With a shaky breath, I turn the key, feeling the grind of unwilling metal tumblers scraping against the intrusion. A release, an unwilling acquiescence, and the lock falls away.

I pull hard and the massive doors swing open.

Mists meet my gaze, thick like the smoke from a fire, but white like the paving stones, the clouds. I can no longer see mountains when I look through. The vapor cools, swirling to my testing fingertips. A tentative step forward and I am shoved backward by a wind just before I see the other side drop away. Fall into a nothingness, above and below. An emptiness that reflects me.

"What is this place?" I yell into the mist, but it eats my words, deadening them into soundless air. I suddenly I realize my legs bleed from the fall, tiny abrasions welling multiple little pots of impossibility.

MOTHER

The grand old woman who lives within the forest of her room, seemingly lying in a perpetual state of advanced age and helplessness, doesn't fool me. I hear her roars in the night, the scream of animals dying in her jaws. And during the daylight hours, I refuse to investigate her aged face, to see what could have been. Closing my eyes tight, I inhale deeply, willing the thoughts to go so that clarity will return. There are things I must do.

I flip the latches to the old woman's room, sealing her inside, and from within I hear the locks click in response, sealing us out. Perhaps it is too much. Not for the first time, I wonder if I am too guarded, too worried over this inconsistent person. But all the other things that lurk behind doors in this place are not good things, and I cannot see how this old woman could be any different. If anything, perhaps this old woman is the worst of them all.

Or the best.

Opening my eyes, I catch a glimpse of daughter peering from her room; her dark brown eyes are black in the candlelight, filled with questions and worry. For a moment, I see my youth, a time before. The sigh of regret escapes my body before I can stop it.

Good that the girl has someone to be close with, someone in the life of their death. It brings me no joy to lock them away from each other each night. But I know the old woman seems to only thicken the shadows. Without those locks, what lies within her room will spill out and the palace will spill within. These two worlds should not intermingle.

Daughter floats away, melting into the growing nightfall, and I can taste her disappointment. The wishes she doesn't speak. The ones she gives to me with the empty bowls of food she's consumed.

Within my rooms, I breathe. I set the lantern on the floor carefully. Everything itches, my eyes, tongue, and hair. I want to be free.

The otkorum-knotted belt on my robe slides free easily and robes drop to the floor. It is an easy thing to find the otkorum of my skin; these slide free easily as well, ready to be let down for the day to be free of all vestments. Finally loosened, my flesh sags free and I leave it too, as a pile on the floor. Skin made dirty with use and wear. I can't remember what's inside anymore, can't recall all the things I used to want to be. I study the mirror, trying to relearn, to remember. All I find are images of the king stuffed behind my ribcage, stifling my heart. I tilt to peer into my skull, opening the top like a jar, a thing filled with coins. I pull at them, reading the tiny inscriptions stamped onto their surfaces—obligation, responsibility, sacrifice.

Loathing overcomes me, for myself and the emptiness of what I've become.

Duty keeps those we love safe and happy, even as it tears years of health and sanity from those who shoulder its heavy burden. Truthfully, we all crave fulfillment...things that give a reason for our existence. When one dwells in the shadow of duty too long, they will find that fulfillment in insidious ways.

Just as I have.

***

In the morning, I dress again, and am put back together before the lights of the sky return. But I am not grateful for it. I return to the old woman's doorway, unlocking each bolt, undoing each lock. A soft growl answers from the other side of the door.

Only sacrifice ahead of me, and I must see it done.

DAUGHTER

Something flits through the dimming streets. It is dark and angry. A thing of regret.

**

"How are you today?"

Grandmother clasps her other hand over mine, enfolding it into a ball of young and old flesh, her eyes shine. "As well as can be expected. Bah, it doesn't matter. How is the girl? How did she live her life since I saw her last?" she asks, her question blooming like a peony in the late spring sun.

"I've only just seen you yesterday," I say with a grin. It's an old ritual between her and me. Grandmother asking what I had done as if it had been years between visits and I, of course, remind her that I had been here the day before.

"One of these days, you'll have something to tell me," she says, a mask of mischief settling into the wrinkles. I don't know how old she is; to me, she's always looked the same—ancient and frail, but never older than old. I've asked before how Imjin Pavilion came to be, how we three came to be here.

"There are no clear answers," grandmother always said in response. And mother, she never answered me at all, except perhaps to tell me to fetch a cup for tea, or some other task.

Outside the pavilion, the trees grow up and down, then sideways, swaying with the wind. The plants inside the room sway as well, giving a dizzying effect.

"Shall I tell you the next part of the story?" Grandmother asks.

I nod yes, trying to hide the eagerness in my eyes. I am curious. I want to know how the tale ends.

"Good then, now where did we leave off? Oh yes..."

**

When the woman entered the wise man's small house, he had been preparing tea and was not at all expecting visitors. So the woman's brisk entrance jarred him, making him slosh hot tea onto his fingers, and he yelped in pain. As you can see, he was already unhappy at the sight of this woman.

The woman was much too upset to take note and immediately began to tell him about her problem. "Wise man," she said. "My husband has returned from war and is no longer himself. He is angry and violent and makes me afraid." She was almost in tears as she told him this. But the wise man still nursed his fingers and only wished he could drink his tea in peace. Worse, this woman was loud and panicked, things he did not favor in women. He cast a sad gaze at the tea kettle.

"I need your help," she begged. "Please, give me a potion so I can make him the man I married again."

With a frustrated sigh, the wise man informed the woman that he had no such potion, and she should go home and simply make her husband food and try being less loud. Surely being dainty and quiet would make her husband happier and less violent.

Then she began to cry. Now the wise man hated that even more, because he believed women who cried were trying to manipulate him. He quickly thought of a solution to his problem.

"Woman," he said, "there is one potion, but I will need you to fetch one of the ingredients, the most vital part for the potion."

Without pausing, the woman answered, "Anything, please just tell me what it is."

"A tiger's whisker," he said, knowing that such a task would be a fool's errand.

The woman fretted over this, of course, because everyone knew that tigers were violent, angry creatures and would surely eat her up rather than offer any whiskers.

"You could, of course," the wise man said, seeing her hesitation, "just go home and try other ways." He was rather hopeful over this, so he wouldn't have the death of the woman on his hands, because surely any tiger she attempted to retrieve a whisker from would eat this woman up.

The woman hesitated, then drew a deep breath, and readied herself. It was for her husband, after all. The woman quickly agreed and left the wise man's house on her quest for the tiger's whisker.

***

Grandmother dips her chin and looks at me. "Now what do you think about that?"

With a shrug, I say, "I think the wise man didn't really care to help the woman at all and only wanted to drink his tea."

At this, grandmother lets out a loud laugh, revealing her brown and missing teeth. She pats me on the hand before falling into another cackle. Her joy makes me joyful, so I sit and grin while soaking up the wonderful sound of her amusement.

"Ah well, that's an good as answer as any." She leans back on the pillows and closes her eyes. "I am tired today, granddaughter, I don't think I will want to hear your story this visit."

Trying to hide my disappointment, I tuck away the book I brought with me. "I understand," I say, but for moment, I don't move to leave. I cannot pierce the quiet to tell her, to ask her all the questions I have inside of me. All the doubt.

"What is it?"

I look up into her ancient face, the way her cheeks plump against the thin skin of age, the lines that dig into her forehead like the rings of a tree. Each line a season of hardship. Or perhaps they mark seasons of happiness. Shouldn't good things leave marks as well as the bad?

"Who am I?" I say, low and calm.

Her eyes widen; the black irises are pools of ink, assessing me. "No one can be told who they are." She raises a hand toward me. "Because no one else has the right to decide our identity, only ourselves."

"Grandmother, I'm not sure how to learn. I feel..." I wander, trying to find the right word, "adrift."

This makes her nod to herself. "Knowing yourself is just as much about mistakes as it is about success." Her face takes on a grim visage, one filled with pain. "It is time."

"For what exactly?" I ask.

"So much to explain. You must understand that there are many halls and pavilions on the palace grounds. Just as the wife in the story has many options. She could have left her husband, could have hurt him back, could have never told anyone about the violence she suffered." Grandmother continues, "The truth is that sometimes, options are just doors meant to give the illusion of choice. Have you ever tried to open those doors?"

I shake my head. "No, mother wouldn't allow it."

Grandmother sucks her teeth in disapproval. "Mother is difficult. She's scared and worried. The things that look like doors here do not function according to expectation. You must seek out the doors, test them. Open them and finally *know*."

"I can't imagine—"

"That's the problem. You can't imagine."

The deep flame of me licks up; those desires rise within, threatening to crush me with the weight of them. As I get up to leave, grandmother puts a hand over mine and cracks her eyes. "Can you do something else for me?"

"Yes, of course. What is it?"

"Question everything."

***

The next day, I approach grandmother's room as usual. I think of all the stories we've told, trying to let them sink into me. I pass mother's paintings; they shriek with crimson fires and hopelessness. She calls out to me while bending over a new painting. Streaks of blue, in many shades, form unrecognizable shapes.

"You will not go to grandmother today," she says.

The menstruation continues, blood staining my undergarments in splotches of crimson; does it still worry her?

Her words crisp against my spirit, and resentment blooms within me. "Why?" I dare to ask. The heaviness of the iron key pulling at the pouch still pinned to my skirts, and the porcelain shard in a deep pocket.

She doesn't turn or reprimand, she points, pausing between brushstrokes. "Look for yourself."

The door to grandmother's room remains shut despite the unlatched locks on this side. I try to turn the knob, but it might as well be stone, for it doesn't give way. I think about her trapped in her bed, waiting for my visit, and suppress a wave of panic.

She is fine. She's always been fine.

Who locks her side of the door?

"She's not as helpless as you think," mother calls down the hall, sensing my concern.

My cheeks burn and I wish I could shred these paintings. I suddenly hate them with a passion. I'd burn them all if I could.

I force myself to study mother's paintings in turn, imagining them in a fire. Here a family wrenched apart, the father pushed into a storm-ridden ocean until he sinks. This one is called "Lies." In another a woman floats; pieces of her body have been torn away as she remains suspended.

Her mouth opens into a dark cavern of pain, she weeps ceaselessly. It is called "Disobedience."

The heaviness within clangs against my ribs and how I wish I could name the feeling, as if giving it identity would absolve me of it. Thrust it from me. Another painting, the only one she hasn't named, draws and repels me simultaneously. I hate this one the most. Mother tells me she painted it from a photograph, a real thing that happened. Women cut into pieces, soldiers grinning arrogantly at the sight, brandishing their horridness. I once asked her how people could have allowed this to happen.

"Search your heart and you will find the answer," she had said.

I've been searching for a long time and nothing but outrage and sorrow answer back. I finger the shard of pottery still in my pocket, letting the sharp edge push into my thumb. Like a ghost I am faded, destined to wait here by grandmother's door, waiting only to be let in.

Quietly, I pass back down the stairs. I am surrounded constantly by beauty. Everything made with great care, the names of artists can be found on almost everything if I look closely enough. There are special little marks, small pictures, letters, swirls. Even the trees, when I look closely, I find more artist marks. A reminder that this was once a world filled with people. The sharp edges of humanity.

Tiny scratches in the glaze beg for close examination. An artist's mark.

A name. "Jayeong."

MOTHER

I feel as if I am swimming through the reflection of the palace, moving through it slowly, cutting through heaviness. I can still hear his voice, a sound imprinted on my soul, and I hate him for that.

"Wife."

"Don't call me that."

"That's what you are, isn't it? Wife. I made you something by marrying you. Made you strong."

The old fury crawls up my throat. He throws back his head and laughs, full and with abandon, and he gives himself over to mocking me.

The pain still stings.

"One day, I will completely forget you," I mouth into the air.

I wasn't always like this.

Check the locks. I must check them. Lantern in hand, I tread over the cobblestones, holding the light up to each door. Must keep these things from coming out.

He didn't always speak to me this way. At first his amber eyes held longing. I never loved him, he never loved me. But I could have been an asset, a valued thing. Appreciated for giving the choicest parts of myself to his service. Did he ever live for me? Did he ever give for me?

"We can live as husband and wife once again."

"No. You always made promises. Respect. Admiration. For hope and freedom. But you never did these things. Only said words, all the while constructing a prison for me. I gave it all up for you."

"You could have said no."

"Could I have?" On the surface he seems right, but the complexity of reality falls heavy on my mind. We do have choices, but we also have responsibility to those around us. To the kingdom. Or to the mere absence of other choices.

"I made you important," he says.

"You made me empty," I say.

DAUGHTER

I watch mother pace in the streets, lantern held high, face flickering in the tiny, contained firelight. Door after door she checks and rechecks. I can hear her weeping and shouting. I turn away and I see the burned woman hangs half in the shadow of a corner; the scent of charred flesh fills the room. She stares and the lantern-light seems to flicker against what is left of the thing's eyes. One good hand shoots up, pointing at something through the window, toward one of the halls. I look out. Mother soon rounds on the queen's quarters. She's quieted and holds her lantern up once again. The doors to the hall open wide, sucking the darkness into the hollowness of its interior space.

Mother stumbles, almost falling, but soon climbs the stone steps to the entrance. Then the great maw of the hall swallows her into the darkness.

The burned woman opens her mouth and behind her jaws I see flames, a great internal fire licking past lips, charring her further. A finger remains outstretched, showing and insisting I follow.

***

The rectangular hall has loomed in my mind for so long, walls of creamy jade framed in red, a stone staircase calling for use. A deep shade greets me as I reach the top, and immense overhangs of the roof beamed and decorated with many designs in a rainbow of colors. This is right. This is where I should be, where I should go. The feeling permeates my soul, and I am heartened. The doors are recessed into the patio space, two grand wooden things, carved with peony and symbols of balance, then washed in a white so distinct it seems to permeate every pore of the wood.

In early morning light, the doors to the queen's quarters remain thrown open. The part of every story that I know about, where the curious girl can't help herself and because she can't help herself, something horrible happens. But discovering the truth destroys the mirage. If only the wife in grandmother's story had done that, looked closely at her own hopes and dreams instead of only her husband.

I am going to look and I am going to *know*.

Gathering up my chima, I peer into the darkness and step forward. The hall swallows me up, ready to gnash me between its teeth. It will succeed.

The interior that had appeared dark and unfathomable from the exterior brightens as if filled with daylight. Before me is a maze of cream-colored rooms, sliding rice paper doors framed in dark wood. These shift in their grooves, moving into configurations in a kind of restlessness, pushing and pulling at one another, segmenting the space, shaping it into squares, then again moving into a large space before shifting yet again into a hall framed by multiple rooms. The doors appear satisfied with this arrangement and go still, waiting for me to be digested.

I could have come here at any time, could have opened these doors. Why have I not done this thing? Why have I stridden over known ground continuously each day without straying with curiosity? Surely, I know the answer to that, I know the protocol, to work only in seemly expectations. Who put these ideas down upon me? Where have I conjured the permission for only small allowances, if at all?

I move about, slowly into the hall, pushing doors to reveal rooms. One by one, I open to emptiness and finery. Celadon vases and pots adorn corners; lacquered tables, low to the floor, are surrounded by cushions. A room with a grand low bed, carved as if a still living tree, swirling, and looping into four short legs, fitted with pillows and blankets of silk. All things that touch the flesh here are smooth, vibrant, clean. Another room opens and I am startled at first: a regal hanbok, its chima embroidered in gold in painstaking detail, set against dusty blue, a white jeogori displayed in the center of the room. Held up by an unseen form, it seems to present itself, to be seen and admired.

But I move on, eager to get to the heart of the building, to understand what drew me here, what answers would be revealed.

Darkness descends, as if the sun snuffed out. My eyes cannot pierce the shadows of the corners, but I can make out scattered shards of pottery, just like the one I had taken for myself.

A sniffling sound from a corner makes me jump and I let out a yelp, half fear and half surprise. From the shadow a form of a man crawls toward me. Young and dressed practically, creeping in unnatural jerky movements. I try to back away but my back hits the wood wall. *What direction is the doorway? Why has the light in the chamber shifted?* He reaches for me, hands cold against my legs, inching up to my arms, pinning me to the wall. In terror I close my eyes as if I could make the discovery disappear.

His breath emanates a chill against my face. "Jayeong," he whispers. This name stirs from within my fear. "Jayeong," he says again.

Forcing eyes open, his face looms over me like a full moon. Not the terror I thought, but a kind face with a gentleness to his luminous, warm eyes. I know him. My bones ache with longing, discovering a missing part of myself that had been gone for too long.

"I've missed you so," he whispers, and I clutch him to me. Our lips meet and he is chill honey. My warmth does nothing to heat him. I push away in confusion. "What is this?"

"I've waited a lifetime," he says.

"I know you," I say. His face has turned to pain, contorted kindness giving way to something else. Fury.

He laughs. "You know me? Is that all you have to say to someone who has spent a life loving you from afar? Missing you from my arms? Is that what you say to what could have been? Instead, you had to be queen."

His hand envelops mine still holding the shard. "A pottery maker is much too simple for you." He brings his face so close that I see the flecks of amber in his eyes, but they are no longer kind or gentle. I see anger, desperation.

"I did what I was supposed to do. What my family told me." What I mean by this confuses me; the words jump into my throat and out my mouth as if I am possessed. "I believed you had moved on. I heard you married. Had children."

"You were always there in the shadows of my heart. She killed herself, you know, because I could only think of you."

A great sadness overcomes me. "If you allowed her to feel this way, you were not the man I believed you to be."

"You could have been mine, Jayeong." His fury dies and his face turns mournful. "What could have been?" And before my eyes, he shatters, just like the other porcelain of my life. A hundred pieces suspended in the air of hope. The pieces of him fall back to the floor.

The wail emerges from my soul, a knowing sorrow that I can never have this thing, this hope and love. I crawl from the chamber sobbing, half delirious with sorrow. I reach for the discarded shard, holding it tight as I pull myself up, leaning heavily against a wall. Its sharp edges are talons of my pain. I fall into a heap, weeping at the loss of what I cannot remember.

MOTHER

There was once a daughter who dreamed in books and conquered knowledge. She married well, so well that she became the queen of all the kingdom. She had believed she was the star of her story, but soon she only became a gilded container. A pair of hands that sliced herself into pieces over and over. Let them come to the banquet and consume what I am, who I am, until nothing remains.

***

I don flesh and can hear daughter within the palace grounds. Her cries mar out the forever sunlight and bloom of flowers. Hers is a sorrow that challenges this false springtime and I weep, too, along with her. She won't understand, never understands.

I stop; something's not right. For countless hours this perfect plum tree has bloomed and given fruit to us without reservation. But now, the flowers have died, and fruit has scattered over the ground, as if someone has shaken the tree.

I attempt to scoop up one of the fallen fruits, only to have it burst at my touch with sticky-sweet smelling rot. Daughter's cries still echo across the palace grounds, but I can only stare at the remnants of plum flesh in my palm.

I've been disappointed by most things in my life; all things that were promised to be important and great have been empty overtures without substance. I, who have been trained to be a good girl, then a good proper woman. It won me a seat next to the king himself, a place as the highest-ranking woman in the kingdom.

But it meant nothing.

Nothing changes here in the palace.

Nothing, until it all changes at once. And I realize, I have not yet made a painting of a plum.

No. I tell myself. No more. The walls slide about me and I remember where I am. I remember all the loss and what led me here.

This is the queen's hall. My hall. My prison, and daughter's cries are *here* with me.

DAUGHTER

The daughter became the queen and one day a mother. The knowledge rotted away in her head. She had wanted to become a scholar. She had wanted so many things for her life, and not once did she dream of being queen.

***

Into the center of the hall, I push further, still weeping. There seems to be no direction here, an endlessly shifting maze. Another room opens before me. The shape of a miserable wasted man forms, seated upon a cushion at a writing desk. Not that his clothing speaks of his misery; in fact he is dressed quite finely in embroidered silks, with a delicate line of hair above his lip and a plume of a neatly dressed beard. His eyes hold a shifty discomfort that makes them appear watery, as if acrid smoke burns them. Certain lines on his face speak of unhappiness, pushing his features into a perpetual mournful expression. He blinks as if trying to clear the tears, and at the sight of me entering the room, he flushes at first, sweat beading on his brow. A man suffering with some malady of emotion.

Unlike Yehun, this figure appears solid and as real as I. He does not rush for me or speak. The man merely stares as I assess him from the doorway. "Who are you?" I hear myself ask. My mind whirls, trying to place the importance of this final piece of the puzzle.

"Who am I?" the man says bitterly. "The proper question is who are you, and what are you doing in my palace?"

"Your palace?"

The man pushes himself up, a tired and slow gesture. Despite this, he rises to full height, and this makes him seem like an immovable tower. Golden robes against golden skin, he takes me in as if I am a mere door...a thing that stands in his way. I don't like the feeling, not at all. I rather liked him sitting and miserable; now I feel control slipping away.

"Have you not wondered, girl, why there is a palace but no king? Why there is finery but no one to impress?"

"Of course, but—"

He raises a hand. "You may answer yes or no."

A burning flush rises to my face, and I nod, casting my eyes down. "Yes," I barely whisper, a mere movement of my lips in acquiescence.

"I am king. Trapped in this hall. Locked in and kept away from my rightful place in the afterlife."

My ears perk and I dare to lift my eyes. "What do you mean by this?"

"My wife refuses her place below me. Serving me." He stares. "You resemble her. Who are you?"

The question startles me, confuses, and I know that I should have an answer. But there is an unfathomable darkness within that only speaks words spoken into it, an interior tunnel of black. Blinking, I lower my eyes instinctively, but the truth tumbles out with a sharp sting. "I do not know."

"You do not know?" he demands, his voice rising like a storm, sharp and sure of his commands.

"I haven't thought." I hesitate, still trying to understand why I do not have an answer to such a simple question. "It's like my identity has flitted away so long ago I can't even remember when it happened. Now, I am only known as daughter."

"Whose daughter then?"

"Mother's daughter."

An aura of distinct fury surrounds us—if the man could exude fire, it would burn me now in this spot. He doesn't speak.

"I am sorry, I don't have answers. That's why I'm here, really. To find them. I need to escape this place. You called it the afterlife? What do you mean?" I peek through the curtain of my hair.

His sudden laugh makes me jump. "You don't know, do you?" His deep amusement calming. "You really have no idea. Girl, look at me."

For a moment I'm not sure if he's testing me, seeing if he can tickle out disrespectful behavior. But no, his tone has slipped back into fatigue, and I raise my eyes, staring into the darkness of his stern face.

"You are dead. I am dead. This place we are, girl, is the tomb that holds our essence."

My mind reels and I gawk, like a small child. *Dead.*

The mist outside the gate, the nothingness. The empty palace grounds. "How?" I manage to eke out.

The king studies me. "How you died?" Is that sadness in his voice I hear? Regret? "I do not have that knowledge. It seems more important we find out how you came to be here in my palace at all."

He takes a step toward me and I back away without thinking, making him halt in midstride. "Palaces are places for kings and queens, not nameless girls. You should not be here."

I can't help but feel the rightness of his words, a truth to the harsh arrogance. *I shouldn't be here, but if not, where should I be?*

"A palace can exist without a king," mother's voice booms through the room.

The man's face grows timid. "Come out, witch woman."

A rice paper door slides open, and she seems to float toward us, mother, wearing the hanbok I saw earlier. A regal gown, a royal thing. Queen, my mind tells me, warns me, tugging insistent at the knowledge.

"You think a palace needs a king, but it doesn't need you at all. Doesn't see you or me, for that matter."

"I made you—"

Mother holds a hand up. "You destroyed everything I could have been. Destroyed my chances at happiness. In return, you gave me duty and sorrow. But it wasn't only you."

The image of yangban men rises to the surface, sitting on the other side of the screen. "She can't," they intone together.

The king doesn't speak.

Doors slide open and close around us, new configurations, rooms filled with people, then gone. Rooms empty of everything but a teapot, then gone. One of the paper doors rattles hard; fragments of something puncture the paper and fall to the floor, broken porcelain. The pottery fragment lets loose a shiver as if awakening in my pocket.

"Please," a rough voice calls, so low I'm sure I've imagined it. "Please." The voice sounds again, an echo of the potter. "Jayeong." A whisper.

Mother doesn't look at me; her face twists in sorrow.

The man had called me Jayeong and I loved him. It is right, the name, for so long I have only known myself as daughter. A name of relationship, dependent on another, never singular or solitary in identity. Are we not defined by our relationships? I ponder these questions with heaviness. How does a woman know herself devoid of human connection? Like the wife in grandmother's story. What was *her* name? What did she think of herself? What do *I* think of myself?

I loved him. Or still do, perhaps? Are we not also defined by love?

I have loved and been loved and even that fell away. Unable to be realized, kept apart by decorum and my family's ambition for me. I put my heart aside. Again, to be a good girl, a good proper woman.

I married the king. Risen to such heights of importance. Finery on my person and all about. Great halls of comfort, beautiful objects, fine food, servants. I would be lying if I said it did not please me, because at first I was quite pleased. Tickled at the attention, admiration, the easy way my wishes could be fulfilled.

The king, my husband, made promises in my bed while I was new and exciting. But men are fickle, and women are without choices.

I hold memories of a time when there were so many more doors and pathways between those doors. So many possibilities for a life. The ones I opened yielded only empty chambers, or weren't doors at all, but false ones that opened to walls. One after another. Soon, I pass other doors with fear, and an ache so deep that I cannot breathe.

I recall slippered feet treading on the wood bridge over the lotus flower pond, the wood bridge to the pavilion that adorns the center island. A small pavilion, but rising high enough for two levels of narrow space. I make landfall; terraced green grasses welcome my steps toward the pavilion entryway. The large door is painted green with swirling delicate designs in white.

My breath hitches, fear injects into my stomach. *Pull it open. Come on now. Just pull it open.* Cold iron meets my hand, a smooth ring attached to a short chain. I take a breath and pull. The door swings as if it's been well-oiled, only the slightest whisper of metal hinges. This time, no wall greets me.

"Jayeong."

I would have given everything to marry Yehun, to have lived as the wife of a master potter. Yet I was chosen for "something greater," my family had said. Something more important.

They didn't tell me the truth. There is nothing great or important about becoming nothing but a container for the king's child.

Over and over, I conceived, and over and over I lost them all. Some as rushes of blood before I knew they existed. A few after my belly protruded with their growth, equal to the size of my hope. One who lived to be born, only to die within months into life. I couldn't even have one thing to be mine.

I was nothing but the king's wife, the vessel who held only emptiness and failure. Soon, I could no longer remember my name. Only wife or queen or daughter-in-law. No one knew my mind or spirit. Least of all the king. My husband. By this time, he had accumulated many concubines and his promises of perpetual passion were now said on other pillows to new and more interesting flesh. He cooled so quickly that there had not even been a stage of moderate affection; only everything, then nothing.

Like losing children.

A faint noise, just barely discernible...a baby's cry. I step inside, trembling and gripping the key. In the corner an ornate cradle hangs suspended from the beams above. The cry comes again and my heart leaps. Removing my slippers, I set them by the door and hurry to the child. Within I find her, awake and alive and beautiful. This is *my* child. My child. I know it is. A daughter.

The room fills with the sound of infants babbling. There are more babies, on the floor, all reaching for me. All mine. There are two sons and another daughter. My children, my sweet innocents.

They cry in unison. I rush to them, scooping up one of my sons, and his tiny form crumbles like sand in my arms. Sucking air in gasps, I try to pick up the others, and each, again, crumbles into sand. *I can't lose them again.*

Running to the cradle, the infant locks her gaze deep into my heart and gurgles. Solid. My heart leaps with joy, relief. At least I will be permitted to have this one, only this child. I can find solace in that. I pull her to me, close, soft plump arms and legs. Warm and perfect, she snuffles into the crook of my arm. At least she and I will be together. I murmur comforting sounds. We can escape together. I'll take her somewhere she can grow to know herself, where she will always know her name.

I step through, back into the day. But something is wrong. This daughter crumbles into sand in my arms. Particles of my heart, just melting away, and behind me, the door slams shut.

The world fades, and I am standing still with the king in a room of mirrors. Each one I turn to I see mother's face. My face.

The king gazes upon the shifting doors. "I've tried to leave many times. Punched holes in the paper. Destroyed many things. But they righted themselves, mended each day when I woke. I could never penetrate the maze to find my way out. Always a loop, forever traveling over the same thing and for nothing. I shouldn't have expected any different for a woman's quarters."

A women's inner world. An infinite loop. All women's lives seemed this way, just like this building. Caught in webs created for us, then supported by us. Why do we torture ourselves this way? Why are we not the kings?

Abruptly I turn away, sliding open the door that leads to another, and I am sliding open a million doors. Yehun is there. "I loved you," he calls desperately, clinging to my ankle. "Why did you leave me?" I break away. Another door slides open, another room, filled with infants, and they cry in unison. So loud they speak in one note of need. I want to help them all, save them all, but they are already crumbling into the dust of my mind.

"Women should know their place. You'll learn that, wife."

What is my name? What is my place?

The burned woman glides toward me. Her face is my face. "You should know your place." Men with masks plunge their swords into my body. "I am the queen," I say. The burned woman wails, but the sound comes from my own mouth. I am sticky with blood. The fumes of gasoline become overwhelming, but nothing can compare to the pain. "You were in the way," they say as the flames eat my fine robes.

"I created a way," I say, the effort flaking charred flesh around me like black snow. Suddenly, I am twirling like a leaf falling from a tree, spinning out of control until I hit the ground.

The king fades until only his robes remain, suspended in the air as if on display. Royal vestments. Mine. These should belong to me. The mirrors see me, lines around my eyes, a gentle sorrow to the deep brown of them.

"Take what is yours."

My body changes, elongates, the shimmer of scales growing over arms, sinuous snake-like, and I burst forth, leaping into the air, through the tiled roof and into the sky. But I cannot climb higher, no higher than the walls, before I begin to fall back down. The palace blurs with so many colors and I slip into the spaces between thoughts. Then my body shatters the surface of the lake, a million particles broken open for me, sucking me down into its eternal eye.

MOTHER

He didn't need to use his fists. It was done one day at a time, each moment sucked away. It wasn't just me. Each of us women who served him, wife and concubines, gave themselves to him. Pinning their hopes and dreams, building waterfalls of love and loyalty, and he drained us all.

I was once young and filled with possibility. I was once daughter, as I should have been grandmother. The palace shuttered it away, made each breath I drew to be about the needs of a great man. They say kumihos are women, but I know the truth, they are men. Not supernatural, but the system that feeds not only upon the wombs of women, but the labor, love, tears. The very spirit of our existence. It is a system that kills us slowly, then curses us for fading at all.

Those men...if I hadn't been the queen, hadn't been his wife, I never would have become the burning woman.

If I had married Yehun, it would have been the same, just a different container, just as the woman he did marry found out. Lives sucked away. Lives lived never for the woman herself but in service to a system made to consume them. A place where women must give respect to men who are without accomplishment or quality, where men must have full acknowledgement for half-done deeds, while in the bedroom require simultaneous surrender and mothering. No, I do not think I wish to give into this system ever again. No love is worth the risk of the slow murder of my spirit.

GRANDMOTHER

There must be a certain balance for the flow of ki, a compliment of wind, water, and earth. Lines that run across the land, reaching into homes, towns, and the great palaces of the Joseon kings. Pungsu is geomancy, the advantageous placement of things within existence. Welcome ki, find ki, guide it to fill life. It's the difference between bad luck and auspicious landscapes. Bad luck and auspicious people.

I think I have been both. Once placed expertly to life, auspicious, ki misting around me. Fortuitous, one could say. Then I have been forgotten, thrown haphazard into life, uncared for. Empty. Bad luck. I am not sure on what note I will end. An end within the beginning. A beginning with the flames.

I am calling to her. Asking her to return. Because in many ways, it is never too late.

DAUGHTER

"How does the story end, grandmother? What became of the wife?"

They say the woman waited each day by the tiger's lair, offering food, acclimating the tiger to her presence. After a long time, the woman was able to get close enough to pluck a single whisker from the tiger. This she brought to the wise man in triumph. 'I have brought the whisker, ahjussi. I am ready for the potion now.' The wise man had all but forgotten about this woman. Of course, there was no potion. Licking his lips, he told her, "You have no need for a potion, you have already tamed a tiger. Perhaps your husband isn't much different. Go to your husband and offer him food. Move slowly. Play dead. Forgive everything when he loses his temper." The wife stood stunned before the old man, not because of any great truth, but because she only then realized he was not a wise man at all, but just a man like any other. So, the wife cocked her head. "I did not tame the tiger. I became the tiger." Her form blurred as she transformed into the great striped beast that roared at the man who once thought so little of the woman, who now could think of nothing but this tiger-woman before him. Of course, the first thing the tiger-woman did was eat up the old man. The second thing she did was eat up her husband. The third and final thing, she remembered her name.

"What was her name?"

Grandmother blurs and I see her smile in the air, then I see the teeth of a great cat. Her flesh fills into stripes; the sinews and muscles of her power replaces the frail, human form.

"I think you know her name," grandmother-tiger says.

"Jayeong," I say, "you."

"Us," she replies, stalking around the great collection of potted greenery. "Me. You. Mother. We are the same, us three. The same but at separate aspects of our life. You see, we needed to learn, to face the prospect of the tiger, to become her as what was meant to be. It's been a long journey."

I nod. "Yes, it has."

"Look," she says through long teeth.

As I peer closely at the forest within her room, I can see it for the first time, truly see, the path between the trunks. My feet know the way; trees have broken from their pots here, their roots growing through cracks, plunging into the wood floor, drinking deep of the energy of the pavilion. Soon, I am no longer walking on wood, but dirt and fallen leaves. Before me swirls great energy, vibrant with red, blue, and yellow lights, spinning and swirling together and apart again. The three together—heaven, humanity, and earth.

"You are heaven. When we are born, we fall from lofty places into our humanity. But that is not the end. Even as we sink into the earth and rot away. That is not the end either. Do you see it?"

The truth of it hits me—the pain of disappointment, of a life lived for others and the waste of it. The waste of giving only to be consumed.

"Why does this happen? Why must we fight like this even in the afterlife to know our womanhood? To be free?"

The tiger stalks around me, blurring again until I see grandmother's form standing next to me. "I suppose to see if we believe it's worth fighting for."

"Worth being reborn for?" I ask, a knowing smile curving my lips.

"Oh yes," she says.

"Good."

I gaze at the gateway, readying myself. I know what I will take into my next life. It will be all my struggles, my will.

Important people, husbands, fathers, the world, will no longer bestow me with worth. Life contains much better ways to die. Better ways to live.

I am power. The power I didn't know I had, wasn't allowed to develop. That which I knit into my soul, the vessel grown for the benefits of others. A name obscured and forgotten against yours. No more will I be a mere identity created from the rib of a man. The secondary to the primary.

I am first and whole and full and forged from my own fires.

I know all this now.

I will imprint the knowledge on my soul, and as I am born again and with it, I will break the world.

As grandmother pushes me, I feel us all fall into each other simultaneously. We are one. I am whole.

I think of walls.

I think of being contained.

Then I think of tearing it all down.

***

My soul is wind and water, and the tiger has taught me to run—away from the stillness and expectations.

***

A baby cries in the hospital room, her small voice determined and strong, and it brings her mother great joy to hear.

"My daughter." The words of a prayer.

"I've waited so very long for you."

LIST OF KOREAN TERMS

ahjussi   older man (addressing respectfully).

chama   endure.

chima   skirt.

deegut   the shape of the Korean character that resembles an angular English "c".

halmoni   grandmother.

hanbok   traditional dress that includes a full skirt and jacket.

jeogori   jacket that is part of traditional dress

ki   Korean word for the Eastern concept of life energy, or the vital force of someone's spiritual existence.

kumiho   fox spirit in Korean lore known for eating livers.

otkorum   traditional knot used to fasten jeogori.

Pungsu   Korean geomancy.

soju   liquor made from rice, wheat, or barley.

sseunami   Korean word for tsunami.

Yangban   class of noble families involved in ruling.

ABOUT THE AUTHOR

K.P. Kulski is a Korean-American author born in Honolulu, Hawaii. A wanderer by requirement and later by habit, she's lived in many places in the United States, as well as two years in Northern Japan. Never one to settle for long, K.P. has embarked on many career adventures, including the U.S. Navy and Air Force, video game design, and history professor. She's the author of the gothic horror, *Fairest Flesh*, from Strangehouse

Books, and *House of Pungsu,* from Bizarro Pulp Press. Her short fiction has appeared in various publications, including *Fantasy* and *Unnerving Magazine,* and anthologies *The Dead Inside,* from Dark Dispatch, and *Not All Monsters,* from Strangehouse Books. She now resides in the woods of Northeast Ohio with her husband and children. Find her at garnetonwinter.com and on Twitter @garnetonwinter.

CPSIA information can be obtained
at www.ICGtesting.com
Printed in the USA
BVHW041344230922
647840BV00006B/231

9 781685 100612